To every child who
sees the world a little differently

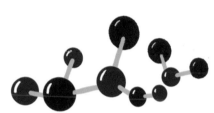

Copyright © 2020 by Ashley Spires

All rights reserved. Published in the United States by Crown Books for Young Readers,
an imprint of Random House Children's Books, a division of Penguin Random House LLC, New York.

Crown and the colophon are registered trademarks of Penguin Random House LLC.

Visit us on the Web! rhcbooks.com

Educators and librarians, for a variety of teaching tools, visit us at RHTeachersLibrarians.com

Library of Congress Cataloging-in-Publication Data is available upon request.
ISBN 978-0-525-58144-4 (trade) — ISBN 978-0-525-58145-1 (lib. bdg.) — ISBN 978-0-525-58146-8 (ebook)

The text of this book is set in 15-point The Cat's Whiskers.

The artwork for this book was rendered digitally, sprinkled with sparkles, and frozen solid.

Book design by Nicole de las Heras

MANUFACTURED IN CHINA
10 9 8 7 6 5 4 3 2 1
First Edition

FAIRY SCIENCE
SOLID, LIQUID, GASSY

Ashley Spires

Crown Books for Young Readers
New York

While the other fairies wish on stars, Esther conducts experiments.
While they learn spells, she studies the law of density.

She's a fairy who prefers a microscope to a wand.

Esther is dedicated to science.
She and her friends use the scientific
method to explore the world around them.

First they ask a question.

What happens to ice when it warms up?

Then they do some research.

DON'T LICK IT!

They each make a hypothesis.

They do experiments, and they examine their results.

Finally they draw their conclusions.

Esther and her friends try to share their discovery at school, but none of their fairymates are interested.

So, as you can clearly see, the rising temperature causes the water to change from solid to liquid, which is the real reason the ice melts!

They are too busy planning for the Magic Fair to listen to her silly logical theories.

Now, Esther, we all *know* that moon sneezes are what make the ice disappear each spring.

PIXIEVILLE MAGIC FAIR!
FUN! AMAZING! SPARKLY!

MAGIC FAIR SIGN-UP:
1. Blossom
2. Thistle
3. Basil
4. Spook
5.
6.
7.
8.
9.
10.

Last year's fair didn't go well for Esther. It turns out magic enthusiasts are surprisingly clueless.

While her fairymates work on their magic projects,
Esther focuses on solving scientific problems.

How does the compass needle always point north?

Last one in the pond is a rotten toadstool!

And there is no bigger problem . . .

SPLOOOT!

. . . than a missing pond!

There are lots of ideas about what happened to the pond.

But only Esther and her science pals observe the facts.

Fig asks a question.

Clover does some research.

Esther forms a hypothesis.

Together, they conduct experiments
and examine the results.

At last, they draw their conclusion.

Since there is no scientific way to force it to rain, Esther and her friends just have to wait to see if her theory is correct.

I've noticed that science seems to involve a lot of waiting.

Come here, pondy pond!

They wait and wait and wait a little longer, until finally it starts to pour.

And, it gives Esther the perfect way to bring science to the Magic Fair!

MAGIC FAIR TODAY!

COLORS AND THEIR MEANINGS

WHAT YOUR AURA SAYS ABOUT YOU!

PIXIE DUST: What Can't It Do?

HOW FATE WORKS. Why I Was MEANT to Write This Report

My Aunt TOOTH FAIRY: The Story of a Molar Hoarder

Has Esther finally made everyone excited about science?

Apparently, the Magic Fair isn't ready for science.
But the judges appreciate a good costume.

Esther may not have won any trophies, but like all good scientists,
she knows that discovery is the best reward.

And there is *always* something new to discover.

ESTHER'S RAINY-DAY EXPERIMENT

You don't have to be a fairy to do a science experiment! Why not make it rain indoors? You'll need these things:

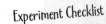

Experiment Checklist

Hot Water
One Large Glass Bowl
Food Coloring
Salt
One Small Glass Cup
Plastic Wrap
Ice Cubes
Spoon

First, pour the hot water into the bowl so it is about a quarter full. Ask an adult for help.

Add food coloring and a pinch of salt to the water and give it a stir.

Next, place the small cup into the bowl. Be careful to keep the cup dry inside.

Quickly cover the bowl with plastic wrap and place a few ice cubes on top.